with
Reading

The Magic SCOOTER

By Julia Jarman

illustrated by Sam Hearn

W

FRANKLIN WATTS

LONDON•SYDNEY

CHAPTER 1
The Birthday Present

It was Caspar's birthday and he had
to go to school.

"But Mum, I want to ride my new scooter!"

He hadn't had time to look at it properly.

There were lots of interesting gadgets

on the handlebars.

"You can ride it to school, Caspar," said Mum. So he did – super fast.

Then he had to leave it in the scooter-park.

He couldn't stop thinking about it!

In class, Lucy suddenly gave him a nudge.

Miss Grundy was staring at him.

"Well, Caspar?"

"Scooter!" said Caspar, as it was the first

word that came into his head.

Everyone laughed.

"I don't think the Romans

had scooters, Caspar."

"They have got scooters in Rome!" cried Simran. "They're called Vespas and they sound like giant wasps…"

"That's modern Rome, Simran! We are doing Ancient Rome," replied Miss Grundy.

Caspar remembered they were studying the Romans. It was quite interesting but he couldn't stop thinking about his scooter…

Miss Grundy held up a picture of a round building with lots of seats, a bit like a football stadium. "What is this?" she asked.

"It's where they did chariot racing," said Lucy.

"And gladiator fights!" added Simran

Miss Grundy nodded. "Yes, it's the Circus Maximus where they held all sorts of games. Now imagine you are a Roman going to see something in the huge arena. I want you to describe exactly what you see. Remember that Rome was a very dangerous place – and beware of thieves!"

Caspar was still thinking about his scooter. Thieves! What if a robber was trying to steal his scooter at this very moment? Caspar stood up and the teacher didn't notice. He walked to the door and she still didn't notice...

"Where are you going?" asked Rosie, the nosiest girl in school.

"To the toilet," said Caspar, quickly.

He did go to the toilets, but then went past them into the playground. He ran on to the scooter-park. Phew! His scooter was still there. The scooter looked cool. The metal bits gleamed. But what were all the dials and gadgets for? Some of them were flashing. He glanced at the other scooters. His looked different.

Caspar had to have another ride. Checking that no one was looking, he gripped the padded handlebars. He put his foot on the platform and pushed off with his other foot.

CHAPTER 2
A Flying Scooter!

"Wow!" He shot forward but a cat ran right

in front of him. "Oh no!

Out of the way, cat!"

Caspar put his foot on the brake,

but he didn't even slow down.

In fact, he went faster.

"OUT OF THE WAY, CAT!"

Caspar closed his eyes, sure he was going to squish the cat, but instead he felt the front wheel leaving the ground. Then he felt the back wheel leave the ground. Suddenly the cat was below him.

At first he thought he was doing a wheelie
and prepared to hit the ground as he came
down. But the scooter didn't come down.
His amazing scooter kept going –
up and up and up!

Caspar glanced over his shoulder.

Fire was streaming out behind him.

His scooter was jet-propelled!

Now the school was far below him.

What was happening? Where was he going?

Caspar felt cold and clammy as he whooshed through a layer of cloud.

Soon the clouds were below him.

When Caspar looked through a gap in the clouds he could see the Earth. It was spread out like a map beneath him. One country after another appeared and disappeared as he flashed past.

Desperately he studied all the gadgets in front of him. He hit one which he thought said HOME.

Then he felt a very strange sensation. It was as if he had a whirlpool in his head.

Caspar didn't know it, but he was travelling through space and time. He was hurtling into the past on his magic time-travelling scooter. But *where* was he going?

CHAPTER 3
Destination Rome

As the whirlpool sensation stopped, Caspar could see a long narrow country below him. It was like a long leg. Down, down, down he went. He was heading for a big hill...

...BUMP! Luckily his scooter had excellent shock absorbers! At first he couldn't see anything because he was surrounded by dust. There was a roaring in his ears, like the crowd at a football match. When the dust settled he saw a sign. He knew where he was!

CIRCVS MAXIMVS

The roaring was coming from inside the stadium. But there was a crowd outside too, staring at him. Some were wearing short tunics, some were in togas.

Caspar realised he was in Ancient Rome!

Caspar scooted over to the entrance.

"You can't go in there," said a guard.

"You're not a Roman citizen. What are you, a barbarian?"

Caspar realised he must look very odd in his modern clothes and he didn't know what to say.

Then one of the crowd dropped to her knees.

It was a girl.

"Can't you see? He must be the god Mercury.

I saw him descend from the sky."

Now the crowd was murmuring. "What

does she know? She's only a slave girl."

Some looked at Caspar puzzled, others gazed at his scooter and its flashing lights. But a few of the people dropped straight to their knees. Mercury? Could it be? Has the god really come down from Olympus?

The girl stepped closer to Caspar.

"Please help me," she whispered.

"My brother Brix is in there."

She pointed towards the arena.

"He is a Gaul like me. We were captured by the Romans and sold as slaves. I am a house slave but Brix was forced to be a gladiator!"

"He has to fight wearing a deadly helmet that he can't see out of," she said sadly. "He will surely die unless you can save him."

Me? thought Caspar. But how? He wished he hadn't come. He wanted to go home. This was far too dangerous.

"Brix has to fight a Retiarius – they are armed with a trident and a net to catch their opponent. But Brix will have to fight blind and rely on his hearing," said the girl.

"Oh no," Caspar gulped.

"He doesn't stand a chance."

"He does if you help! The crowds think you are Mercury, one of their gods. Please help him," begged the girl one last time. Caspar glanced round. The man at the gate was bowing on his knees. But another man was looking at Caspar suspiciously.

Caspar took a deep breath.

WHOOSH! He scooted past the gatekeeper, under the arch and into the arena.

The suspicious-looking man tried to follow, but the gatekeeper blocked his way.

CHAPTER 4
Rescue Mission

At first no one noticed Caspar, so he had a few moments to survey the scene. The seats were packed with hundreds of shouting spectators – including Emperor Nero!

Suddenly there was an enormous roar as the gladiators entered the arena. They bowed to the Emperor and then took out their weapons.

"Hurry, they're about to start!" urged the slave girl. She had sneaked in behind Caspar and was hiding behind a pillar.

An official raised his hand.

There was silence.

"Let combat begin!" he ordered.

The two gladiators stood facing each other
in the sandy arena, weapons raised.

It was so unfair, thought Caspar, but what
could he do? He thought hard. The arena
was surrounded by a high wall. He would
have to do a wheelie over it, but he needed
a good run up for that. And then what?

The gladiators started to circle each other. Brix tilted his head slightly to one side, listening for movement. The Retiarius moved stealthily, trying not to be heard.

Then he stepped forward swiftly, aiming the net over Brix's head. Brix jumped back out of reach. He was very nimble.

The Retiarius was sneaky. He whirled the net round Brix's head. He thrust the trident towards his arm. The sharp prongs of the trident drew blood, but Brix still jumped out of the way.

Caspar began to make a plan. He studied the gadgets on his scooter.

When he looked up again the net was on the ground. Brix was jumping over it, sword at the ready.

He closed in on the Retiarius and drew back
his arm, about to strike a blow. Suddenly
the crowd gasped: "Lion!"

Someone had let a lion into the arena. It
was sniffing the air. It got a whiff of blood
and rushed towards Brix, jaws open wide.

Caspar went into action. He did a wheelie over the wall. He scooted towards Brix. The Retiarius had wasted no time. He had grabbed the net and flung it over Brix. The lion was only seconds away...

Caspar swooped low. He grabbed the net, wrenching it from the Retarius's grasp. He hit the button saying HOME, not ROME. He got it right this time and the scooter started to rise.

CHAPTER 5
Destination Home

Phew! Would the magic scooter really get him home? Not yet. There was something else he had to do.

"My sister, Trixi," muttered Brix, "please save her too." Caspar could see her waving in the arena, happy that her brother was safe.

"Please," said Brix. "I am sure you can find Gaul. You could take us home."

There was chaos below. Some people were angry. They had wanted to see someone killed. Some were astonished. Had the god come down from Olympus and rescued the gladiator? What did this mean?

Caspar took a deep breath.

He pressed DESCEND.

"Come on!" he yelled to Trixi as he landed beside her. She jumped on.

Caspar pressed ASCEND. Up they zoomed.

Caspar spelled out GAUL on the keyboard.

Soon they were flying over France.

"Look, there's our village!" cried Trixi.

Caspar pressed DESCEND. The villagers were thrilled to see Brix and Trixi. "It's all thanks to Caspar," they said. "He's a real hero."

They begged him to stay for a feast, but Caspar knew he had something else to do. He waved goodbye and pressed HOME.

ZOOM! He felt the strange sensation again, as if he had a whirlpool in his head. Caspar was travelling through space and time. He was hurtling forward on his magic time-travelling scooter.

Soon, when the whirlpool sensation stopped,
he recognised some landmarks below.
There was his country. There was his town.
There was his school.

"Phew!" gasped Caspar as he landed
in the playground.

"You were gone a long time," said Rosie.

"I had things to do," said Caspar, smiling.

Now he was going to write the best

description of the Circus Maximus ever.

He didn't tell Rosie about his magic

scooter ride. In fact he didn't tell anyone.

He just looked forward to his next

time-travelling adventure.

First published in 2014 by
Franklin Watts
338 Euston Road
London
NW1 3BH

Franklin Watts Australia
Level 17/207 Kent Street
Sydney
NSW 2000

Text © Julia Jarman 2014
Illustration © Sam Hearn 2014

The rights of Julia Jarman to be
identified as the author and Sam Hearn as
the illustrator of this Work have been
asserted in accordance with the Copyright,
Designs and Patents Act, 1988.

Series Editor: Melanie Palmer
Series Advisor: Catherine Glavina
Series Designer: Cathryn Gilbert

A CIP catalogue record for this book is
available from the British Library.

ISBN 978 1 4451 3353 9 (hbk)
ISBN 978 1 4451 3354 6 (pbk)
ISBN 978 1 4451 3355 3 (ebook)
ISBN 978 1 4451 3356 0 (library ebook)

Printed in China

Franklin Watts is a division of Hachette
Children's Books, an Hachette UK company
www.hachette.co.uk